BATMAN™
BATTLES
MR. FREEZE

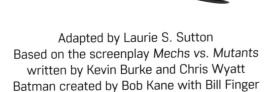

Adapted by Laurie S. Sutton
Based on the screenplay *Mechs vs. Mutants*
written by Kevin Burke and Chris Wyatt
Batman created by Bob Kane with Bill Finger

Simon Spotlight
New York   London   Toronto   Sydney   New Delhi

SIMON SPOTLIGHT
An imprint of Simon & Schuster Children's Publishing Division
1230 Avenue of the Americas, New York, New York 10020
This Simon Spotlight edition May 2017. All rights reserved, including the right of
reproduction in whole or in part in any form. SIMON SPOTLIGHT and colophon are
registered trademarks of Simon & Schuster, Inc. For information about special
discounts for bulk purchases, please contact Simon & Schuster Special
Sales at 1-866-506-1949 or business@simonandschuster.com.
Manufactured in the United States of America 0617 LAK
10 9 8 7 6 5 4 3 2
ISBN 978-1-4814-9179-2 (hc)
ISBN 978-1-4814-9178-5 (pbk)
ISBN 978-1-4814-9180-8 (eBook)

CHAPTER 1

The people of Gotham City were used to seeing some strange things, but this was the weirdest one yet! The entire city was frozen over. Buildings looked like icebergs. A blizzard blew snow through the streets on a *summer's* night.

A few hours ago the weather had been sunny and warm. Now it was arctic. To make matters worse, a terrifying monster stomped through

the streets, towering above skyscrapers. It was Killer Croc, grown to an impossible size.

The Flash and Nightwing raced to save innocent civilians in Croc's path. They paused when they saw another incredible sight: a giant robot Bat-Mech!

"Scanning for target. . . . Acquired," Batman said from the cockpit of the Bat-Mech, and headed for Killer Croc.

The super-villain was surprised when the giant robot smashed into him and sent him reeling. He recovered and returned the attack. The Dark Knight punched the villain with a mechanical fist. Croc staggered backward, but then he rushed the Bat-Mech and pushed it toward a building. The people inside screamed as they fled to safety.

Gotham City became a battleground for the two tremendous titans.

TWO WEEKS EARLIER . . .

It was a warm summer night in Gotham City. Families took time out to enjoy the mild weather. But belowground, in the Batcave, it was business as usual.

Robin studied a file of Batman's greatest foes. He had already encountered the Joker in person, with embarrassing results. As he scanned the holo-displays, the Batmobile roared into the Batcave.

"Studying? Good," Batman told Robin.

"I'm familiarizing myself with your biggest villains," Robin replied. He pointed to an image. "Who's this little guy?"

"Oswald Chesterfield Cobblepot. The Penguin," the Dark Knight answered. "I . . . sent him away for a while."

In a desolate arctic landscape, the Penguin sat in an ice cave and grumbled.

"That cursed Batman. It's all his fault that I'm stranded here," the villain complained to his pet penguin, Buzz. "I should be ruling Gotham City, not stuck in Mr. Freeze's lab of half-working machines."

Suddenly Mr. Freeze entered the lab. He grumbled as he searched for a particular object.

"Solitude! That's all I ask for. And yet my territory has been invaded!" Mr. Freeze complained.

"You mean that new oil drilling platform?" the Penguin asked.

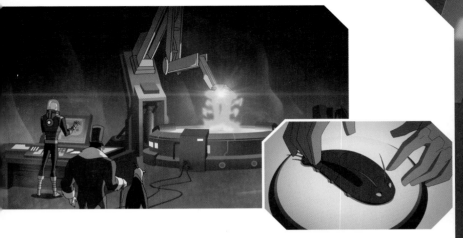

Mr. Freeze found what he was looking for. It was a small triangular pod. The device didn't look like anything important until Mr. Freeze attached it to the back of a small sea creature. The animal grew to tremendous size!

"My monster, attack!" Mr. Freeze commanded. The creature lumbered out of the lab toward the oil drilling platform. "Now, fools, you know the consequences of crossing me, Dr. Victor Fries!"

CHAPTER 2

The massive monster slammed into the drilling rig and toppled it. *BLAM! SMASH!* Workers fled in panic. Some of them ran inside an equipment shed. They came out a moment later driving a Wayne Enterprises drilling machine. The monster was no match against the machine. Mr. Freeze's device was destroyed and the creature shrank back to normal size. As the workers cheered, Mr. Freeze stomped away in bitter defeat. But the Penguin had a plan.

"You want better monsters?" the Penguin asked Mr. Freeze. "I can help. But we have to return to Gotham City."

"To Gotham City," Mr. Freeze agreed.

In Gotham City, Batman attended a Wayne Enterprises technology showcase as Bruce Wayne, Batman's true identity. He gave Damian a break from his Robin training so he could come along. Damian was amazed to see Bruce laugh and socialize with the guests.

"He's so . . . friendly!" Damian gasped.

"Yeah, it freaked me out the first time I saw it too," Oliver Queen remarked from beside the boy.

"Green Arrow!" Damian blurted, accidentally revealing Oliver's secret identity.

Thankfully, no one heard Damian's slip-up. Everyone's attention was on Dr. Kirk Langstrom and the presentation he was about to give. Behind him, a cutting-edge drill mech marched into the spotlight. Dr. Langstrom described its potential uses. As the technician inside the mech used its state-of-the-art Plasma Pincers to melt solid rock, Bruce Wayne received an emergency alert from the Batcave. Someone was breaking into Arkham Asylum for the Criminally Insane!

At Arkham Asylum, Mr. Freeze and the Penguin walked down the cell blocks as if they were at the supermarket. The first on their shopping list was Bane. Mr. Freeze used his Freeze Gun to ice the door's security panel, and the Penguin shattered it with his umbrella. The next was Chemo. Then Killer Croc. And last, Clayface.

"Wait, you don't expect me to work with this snake, do you?" Bane said, pointing to Killer Croc. "He sold me out to the police!"

Suddenly the Penguin was wrapped up in a Batrope and hauled off his feet. Batman, Robin, and Green Arrow faced the villains.

Clayface tried to fool Robin by disguising himself as Police Commissioner Gordon, but Green Arrow saw through the deception. Robin attacked the muddy menace but was thrown across the room. Batman tossed a cable Batarang at Mr. Freeze, but Chemo spewed acid at it and dissolved the cable.

Mr. Freeze used the distraction to ice-blast an escape route in the floor.

"There are sewer tunnels under here," Batman observed. "They had a vehicle waiting. They're gone."

In a secret lair under the waters of Gotham Bay, the villains' plan was about to hatch. Bane, Chemo, and Clayface were hooked up to a massive machine. When Mr. Freeze activated the device, it extracted the chemicals responsible for villains' superhuman strength, hypertoxicity, and ability to stretch. Bane's venom, Chemo's chemicals, and Clayface's mud drained from their bodies into a central container and combined into a new and unique substance. Mr. Freeze poured some of the liquid into a test tube and injected it into Killer Croc. He began to grow to tremendous size!

Minutes later, the waters of Gotham Harbor churned as the monster Killer Croc arose from out of the deep.

"It's time to have a little fun," Croc said, ready to test the effects of Mr. Freeze's formula. He sucked in water from the bay and then blew it out in a blizzard blast!

Snow started to fall on summertime Gotham City.

CHAPTER 3

Gotham City started to freeze. Ice formed around the buildings. Gale-force winds blew snow through the streets. The Batmobile drove through the blizzard, because super heroes did not get snow days.

Killer Croc stomped through the streets of Gotham City, busting down buildings and covering the streets in ice and snow. He paused when he saw the Batmobile.

Batman and Robin saw the enormous villain. Batman did not hesitate. He sped the vehicle straight at Killer Croc!

Suddenly a streak of red raced next to the Batmobile. It was The Flash! Croc blew a blast of ice at the heroes. Cleats popped out of the Batmobile's wheels and kept the car on the road. The Flash slid out of control.

Batman fired missiles toward Killer Croc. *BOOM! BOOM!* Croc took the hits. He was dazed, but he managed to grab the Batmobile and throw it at a nearby skyscraper. The Batmobile was about to hit the building when mechanical wings unfolded from the sides of the car, transforming the Batmobile into the Batwing!

Batman and Robin flew above the scene and soon spotted another threat. A giant-sized Chemo! The villain rose up out of the bay and started to spew ice and snow over Gotham City, just like Killer Croc.

Inside the secret lair, Mr. Freeze watched on-screen as his creations turned Gotham City into an arctic landscape. He was pleased. The plan was working. He was so focused on the sight that he did not notice the Penguin's pet, Buzz, steal a vial of his formula and toss it to the Penguin. Behind Mr. Freeze's back, the Penguin smiled at Bane and Clayface.

Out on the snowy streets of Gotham City, citizens were in danger from the sudden change in the weather. Giant icicles fell from buildings, and snowdrifts turned into avalanches. Green Arrow did his best to rescue people, but he was only one person. It was a good thing he had help—from Nightwing!

Not far away, Batman and Robin battled Chemo in the harbor. Chemo blasted the Batwing with an ice storm. It formed a tornado and flung the aircraft out of control. The Batwing was about to hit the ground! Batman pressed a button on the control panel and the plane transformed back into Batmobile mode. The tires gripped the street as Batman braked to a stop.

While Batman and Robin caught their breath, Commissioner Gordon watched Killer Croc from the roof of the Gotham City Police Department building. Croc was going to smash it! Gordon aimed the Bat-Signal at the monster's eyes and temporarily blinded him. Croc roared and pounded his fists into the building, narrowly missing two police officers. Debris rained down as Croc lifted his mighty fist for another blow. This time The Flash ran to the rescue. He picked up the police officers and carried them to safety. Croc swiped at Commissioner Gordon, but Nightwing swooped in on a grapple and swung him out of danger.

Mr. Freeze gazed at a frozen Gotham City. The snow-covered skyline was beautiful to him.

"Frozen. A wasteland paradise. Everything I've ever dreamed," Mr. Freeze said.

"Cold enough to ditch the suit?" the Penguin asked as he, Bane, and Clayface stood nearby.

Mr. Freeze nodded and pressed a button. His protective Freeze Suit detached and fell away.

"I'm finally free," Mr. Freeze murmured. Then he pointed his Freeze Gun at the Penguin. "And your usefulness is at an end."

CHAPTER 4

"W e're partners!" Penguin protested as Mr. Freeze aimed a Freeze Gun at him.

"I'm no fool. You wanted to return to Gotham City to rule it," Mr. Freeze said. "But now *I* rule it. You'll never get the upper hand on me."

"I already have," the Penguin replied.

That was when Bane and Clayface injected themselves with the stolen vial of Mr. Freeze's formula. Bane and Clayface grew to an enor-

mous size! Clayface smashed the Freeze Gun and tossed Mr. Freeze into a snowdrift five blocks away! Then he lumbered away in search of Batman.

Bane had his own target in mind.

Nightwing and Commissioner Gordon watched Killer Croc stomp away from them. He had recovered from the Bat-Signal being beamed into his eyes and was looking for a target. The Flash zipped to a stop next to Nightwing and Gordon. *THUMP! THUMP! THUMP!* They all turned to see what was coming. Giant-size Bane pounded around the corner and lunged straight for Killer Croc, surprising him with a massive punch.

"Time to settle up, Croc!" Bane boomed.

"Can't say I expected to see that today," The Flash admitted.

"Come on—this is Gotham City," Gordon said.

Not far away, Batman and Robin watched as Croc and Bane battled. With the heroes' attention on the fight, they didn't see Clayface come up from behind them until it was almost too late. *WHOMP!* They flipped and rolled out of the way of Clayface's fist just in time.

"There you are!" Clayface said as he reared back for another blow.

Suddenly Clayface started to change. His gigantic body leaked lava. Then he started to erupt like a volcano!

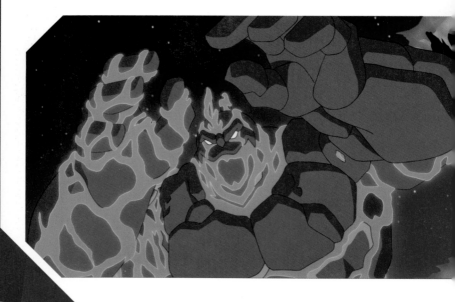

"He's unstable," Batman said. "Whatever Freeze did, Clayface can't handle it." Batman tossed the key to the Batmobile to Robin. "Keep Clayface from destroying the city until I get back," he told his young partner. A few moments later the Batcycle roared up by remote control.

Batman hopped on the Batcycle and zoomed off in one direction. Robin drove the Batmobile in another, but not exactly on purpose. He wasn't familiar with the controls!

Clayface flowed like lava in pursuit of the Batmobile. Robin raced ahead of the igneous monster. He turned a corner to escape and was confronted by a brick wall!

"How did he do plane mode?!" Robin yelled. "Plane mode now!"

The vehicle responded by transforming into the Batwing. Robin pulled up on the controls and launched the aircraft into the sky.

"Oh yeah!" Robin shouted, feeling confident now. He piloted the Batwing into a strafing run at Clayface. "Eat missiles, lava breath!"

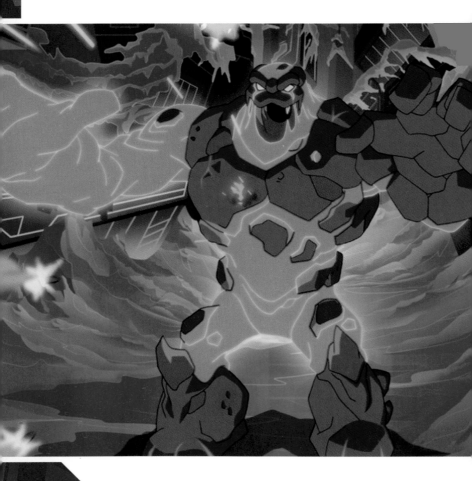

Batman headed back to Wayne Enterprises. His plan to save Gotham City involved a project being developed in a basement workshop. Dr. Langstrom met the Dark Knight in front of the building. They were joined by Green Arrow.

"What are *you* doing here?" Batman asked, surprised to see his fellow hero.

"You'll see," Green Arrow replied.

When the trio arrived in the workshop, a powerful spotlight switched on and illuminated a gigantic robot mech suit—the Bat-Mech! As Dr. Langstrom booted up its systems, a second spotlight revealed a second mech suit—the Green Arrow Mech!

"You ordered your own mech?" Batman asked, surprised again.

"You think you're the only billionaire in the world?" Green Arrow replied with a smile. "Besides, you might need backup."

"Let's go," Batman said as he climbed into the Bat-Mech.

CHAPTER 5

Below Wayne Enterprises a countdown was in progress. Ten . . . nine . . . eight . . .

The Bat-Mech rose up through a launch silo. The ice covering a giant steel hatch cracked open. Seven . . . six . . . five . . .four . . . three . . . two . . . one . . . *ROAR!* The giant robot Bat-Mech launched out of the tunnel, with Batman in the cockpit. A few moments later the Green Arrow Mech followed. But Batman's plan to save the city had only just begun.

"Green Arrow, you're on Chemo. Stop the freezing process," Batman said as he acquired his target—Killer Croc. "Dr. Langstrom, I'm sending you on a special mission."

Bane and Croc ignored everything and everyone else as they battled each other. They smashed into frozen buildings. Croc swung his tail at Bane and connected. *SMAAAAASH!* Bane landed in the middle of a construction site. *BLAM! CRASH!* The unfinished structure collapsed and fell onto Bane, burying him.

"Masked freak: zero. Croc: everything," Killer Croc proclaimed triumphantly, just before the Bat-Mech roared out of the snowy sky.

Elsewhere, Robin fired the Batwing's missiles and machine guns at Clayface. The blasts cracked the monster's outer shell. Liquid lava poured out. It looked like the super-villain was destroyed!

"Oh yeah!" Robin exclaimed in triumph, until the lava gathered together and Clayface re-formed.

Clayface made a surprise swipe at the Batwing. *SMACK!* He connected! The Batwing spun out of control.

In the cockpit, Robin struggled with the unfamiliar control panel. He pushed random buttons, looking for a lifesaving option.

"How did Batman do it?" Robin said with a gasp.

Robin was about to crash when he finally found the right button. The Batwing suddenly reverted to Batmobile mode. Its tires hit the ground and the car skidded to a halt. Robin watched Clayface smash a bridge as the villain stomped away.

"Keep Clayface from destroying the city," Robin grumbled. "Sure. No problem."

Suddenly a voice shouted over the comm unit.

"Robin! Come in!" Dr. Langstrom said. "I'm headed your way! Batman has a plan for dealing with the lava creature!"

In the harbor, the Green Arrow Mech zeroed in on Chemo. Green Arrow aimed the robot's giant energy crossbow at the monster and fired. *ZZBLAAM! ZZBLAAM!* The laser bolts bounced off! The Green Arrow Mech followed up with a good old-fashioned punch. *POWWWW!* Chemo struck back with a massive blow. Huge waves crashed onto the shore as the two giants fought in the bay.

Not far away, back on the roof of the G.C.P.D. building, Robin and Dr. Langstrom hurried to assemble a laser cannon. This was Batman's plan to defeat Clayface. Nightwing and The Flash helped collect parts from all over the city. Nothing like this had ever been constructed. No one knew if it would work—not even Dr. Langstrom, who designed it.

None of them noticed Mr. Freeze watching from the shadows nearby.

CHAPTER 6

Batman and Killer Croc fought a titanic battle. It was mech against mutated monster. Neither of them noticed Bane rise up out of the rubble. Bane grabbed the Bat-Mech from behind.

"I'm going to pry open this shell of yours, Batman, so I can get to the soft center," Bane threatened.

Batman fired dorsal missiles at the super-villain, and Bane went down. The Dark Knight slammed

Killer Croc into the ground. Finally Croc was down for the count.

"Thanks for doing the dirty work," Bane said as he came up behind the Bat-Mech again. "With Killer Croc out of the way, I can enjoy my dominion over Gotham City."

On the rooftop of the G.C.P.D. building, the laser cannon was nearly complete. Dr. Langstrom switched on the device. It hummed, but then the hum turned into a high-pitched whine. *BAM!* Smoke drifted up from the machine.

Suddenly Mr. Freeze stepped out of the shadows. The heroes were surprised and suspicious when Mr. Freeze offered to fix the laser cannon.

"Why?" Robin asked.

"All I wanted was to be left alone in my desolate land, but Penguin convinced me to assault Gotham City," Mr. Freeze admitted. "I was manipulated and betrayed."

Mr. Freeze held up a triangular pod.

"This is one of my arctic devices. Coupled with your cannon, this could be an effective weapon against Clayface," Mr. Freeze said.

"Can we trust him?" Robin asked the other heroes.

At that moment, the Bat-Mech was being held up in the air by giant-size Bane. He was about to snap the robot like a twig, but Batman launched a Batarang and snapped Bane's venom tubes instead. Without the source of his strength, Bane could not withstand the Bat-Mech's blows. Batman knocked Bane unconscious next to Killer Croc. As Mr. Freeze's formula wore off, they returned to normal size.

Batman headed toward the harbor. He arrived to see that Green Arrow was in trouble. The mech was missing one arm, and Chemo was spewing acid at its legs. Suddenly the Bat-Mech gripped Chemo from behind. The villain turned and caught a punch from the Bat-Mech square in the face.

Atop the G.C.P.D. building, the heroes faced the fiery flow of Clayface. Mr. Freeze fired the cannon, and an arctic beam hit the monster! Clayface fought against the assault by throwing blobs of lava. Mr. Freeze was not protected by his Freeze Suit and felt the heat. Chunks of ice spread over Clayface as his body froze inch by inch. At last he froze solid. Mr. Freeze collapsed from the heat, his mission accomplished.

From his crippled mech, Green Arrow watched Chemo battle the Bat-Mech. A massive blow crushed one of the Bat-Mech's arms. Batman disconnected it and replaced it with the crossbow arm from the Green Arrow Mech. He fired the energy weapon at Chemo's chest at close range. A crack formed! The acid goo that was Chemo's real body was exposed at last. The Bat-Mech pounded at the weak spot. Green Arrow left his mech suit and fired explosive arrows directly into the crack.

The blasts opened the crack and dazed Chemo long enough for Batman to deploy a Vacuum Containment Unit to suck the goo into his suit's Collection Chamber. Giant Chemo became a shell of his former self. The final monster had been defeated.

The Gotham City Police rounded up Killer Croc, Bane, and Chemo. "They'll be fine once they wake up back at Arkham Asylum," Gordon said.

"What about Mr. Freeze?" Robin asked. He had retrieved Mr. Freeze's suit for him.

"He'll stand trial for causing this mess," Gordon replied. "It's only fair."

Just then Batman brought in the Penguin, who was left defenseless without his henchmen. "I'll have the last laugh," the Penguin taunted.

"Hey, don't forget his pet!" Green Arrow said as he pushed Buzz kicking and squawking into a police wagon.

With the danger over, the people of Gotham City filled the streets. Children played in the quickly melting snow. Mr. Freeze's artificial winter was no match for the summer heat. No one noticed as a gap formed in the ice encasing Clayface. He slipped out of his prison and into the sewers. The heroes would have to catch him next time!